HAPPY READING!

Mark Collins

Ben's Day!

Story & Pictures by
Mark C. Collins

Edited by G. W. Gentry

Dedicated to all the *only children* who don't
know the meaning of the word "bored."

The first day of Summer, Ben POPS out of bed.
He feeds his fish, Henry, and pats his dog, Fred.

His breakfast is waiting, and smells really yummy
With pancakes and sausage to fill up his tummy.

Ben's dressed now and happy
He's riding outdoors.
His new bike is speedy-
Just watch as he soars!

All geared up for diving
In swim trunks and fins,
Ben takes to the water.
The shark hunt begins!

Ben thinks of his tree house and starts up the ladder,
But changes his mind when he's met with a splatter!

A Summertime shower cleans Ben up fast,
Leaving him puddles where jumping's a blast!

Inspired to fetch his
Colors and brushes,
Ben paints a grand picture
With stylish touches!

Where many "friends" join him
For sandwich and punch.

Back in his "lab" now,
There's much more to do.
Professor Ben mixes up
Green, icky goo!

It's time for a snack
From the truck down the street.
A mountain of ice cream
Is such a cool treat!

Adventure continues,
Just follow the map,
As Captain Ben buries
A treasure out back.

Later, the loot gets returned without qualm
On very strict orders from Admiral Mom.

Ben's up on
The stage now
And rocking
The crowd.
He's dancing
And singing
And playing
So loud!

Mom calls, "Let's eat, Gang!"
It's now time for dinner.
Ben sits up and
Eats his food like a winner.

After dessert,
Ben takes off
In a flash!

Dad stops him,
"It's YOUR turn to
Take out the trash."

With his chores behind him, it's now getting dark.
Ben catches fireflies out in the park.

After he frees them, it's time for Ben's bath.
With oodles of bubbles, he can't help but laugh.

Dressed in
His jammies
And feeling
Quite spent,
Ben hears
A jungle
Outside of
His tent!

It's late now; Ben's tired
And flops into bed,
Then whispers, "Good night, guys"
To Henry and Fred.

The End
(until tomorrow)

About The Author

I began drawing at the age of two, and have wanted to be an artist for as long as I can remember. After graduating from art school, I went through almost two decades as a graphic designer before switching to illustration solely, and since 2001 I've illustrated for textbooks, magazines, packaging, and other authors' books.

Through the course of my life, I've dabbled in poetry, song writing, short stories, and recently took up writing children's books. This is an area where I can combine my writing, design, and illustration skills into fun, colorful works for kids (and adults).

Mark Collins

Mark C. Collins (illustrator) is represented by DEBORAH WOLFE, LTD, and his work can be seen on the web at **IllustrationOnline.com.**

Other books by Mark C. Collins - available on Amazon.com
• Grandma Stinks!
• Meet The Bugs!
• Harry's Hair

Website: markcollinsillustration.com

 facebook.com/pages/Mark-Collins-Illustration/163120997136936

 pinterest.com/mcillustr8r

 twitter.com/KILLUSTR8R

Made in the
USA
Middletown, DE